SandCastle™
Perfect Pets

Terrific Turtles

Anders Hanson
AUTHOR

C.A. Nobens
ILLUSTRATOR

Consulting Editor, Diane Craig, M.A./Reading Specialist

ABDO
Publishing Company

Published by ABDO Publishing Company, 4940 Viking Drive, Edina, Minnesota 55435.

Printed in the United States.

CREDITS

Edited by: Pam Price

Concept Development: Nancy Tuminelly

Cover and Interior Design and Production: Mighty Media

Photo Credits: Brand X Pictures, Comstock, Eri Morita/Getty Images, Zen Sekizawa/Getty Images, ShutterStock, Thinkstock

LIBRARY OF CONGRESS CATALOGING-IN-PUBLICATION DATA

Hanson, Anders, 1980-
   Terrific turtles / Anders Hanson ; illustrated by C.A. Nobens.
       p. cm. -- (Perfect pets)
   ISBN-13: 978-1-59928-755-3
   ISBN-10: 1-59928-755-2
   1. Turtles as pets--Juvenile literature. I. Nobens, C. A., ill. II. Title.

   SF459.T8H35 2007
   639.3'92--dc22

                         2006033254

SandCastle™ books are created by a professional team of educators, reading specialists, and content developers around five essential components—phonemic awareness, phonics, vocabulary, text comprehension, and fluency—to assist young readers as they develop reading skills and strategies and increase their general knowledge. All books are written, reviewed, and leveled for guided reading, early reading intervention, and Accelerated Reader® programs for use in shared, guided, and independent reading and writing activities to support a balanced approach to literacy instruction.

SandCastle Level: Transitional

LET US KNOW

SandCastle would like to hear your stories about reading this book. What is your favorite page? Was there something hard that you needed help with? Share the ups and downs of learning to read. We want to hear from you! To get posted on the ABDO Publishing Company Web site, send us e-mail at:

sandcastle@abdopublishing.com

TURTLES

Turtles are sensitive, solitary, interesting animals. Turtles can be terrific pets if you learn how to care for them properly.

4

Peyton got his turtle at a pet store. He looked for an active, healthy turtle to be his pet.

Turtles should never be dropped. Ms. Palmer shows her students the right way to hold a turtle.

Leslie thinks it's cute when her turtle pulls its head into its shell. But this usually means the turtle is nervous.

Blake feels the underside of his turtle. After handling his turtle, Blake always washes his hands to remove any germs.

11

Adrian keeps his turtle in an aquarium. It has a dry area for basking and a wet area for swimming.

A Turtle Story

Tom was playing
by the pond one day,
when he saw a rock
walking across the way.

15

16

The walking rock
put Tom in shock.
He took a step closer,
and it sniffed at his sock.

Tom said, "Oh, you're
a turtle. Now I see!
Do you want to go
for a ride with me?"

19

20

Tom visits his friend whenever he can. And that's how their terrific friendship began.

Fun facts

Some water turtles hibernate in winter by burying themselves in soft mud at the bottom of a pond or marsh.

The largest turtle is the leatherback turtle. This sea turtle can weigh up to 2,000 pounds.

Turtles cannot crawl out of their shells. Turtles' rib and back bones have evolved over time to form the hard, inner part of the shell.

Instead of teeth, turtles have sharp ridges on their upper and lower jaws. Some turtles, such as the alligator snapping turtle, have a nasty bite. Watch your fingers!

Glossary

active – moving around quickly and often.

bask – to enjoy lying or sitting in the sun.

germ – a tiny, living organism that can make people sick.

sensitive – able to detect or respond to slight changes in condition.

solitary – being or living alone.

student – someone who studies in school or on his or her own.

terrific – very good.

usually – commonly or normally.

About SandCastle™

A professional team of educators, reading specialists, and content developers created the SandCastle™ series to support young readers as they develop reading skills and strategies and increase their general knowledge. The SandCastle™ series has four levels that correspond to early literacy development in young children. The levels are provided to help teachers and parents select appropriate books for young readers.

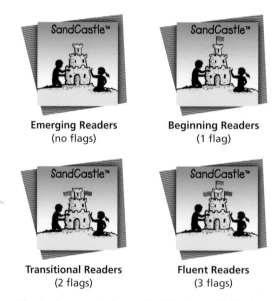

Emerging Readers
(no flags)

Beginning Readers
(1 flag)

Transitional Readers
(2 flags)

Fluent Readers
(3 flags)

These levels are meant only as a guide. All levels are subject to change.

To see a complete list of SandCastle™ books and other nonfiction titles from ABDO Publishing Company, visit www.abdopublishing.com or contact us at:
4940 Viking Drive, Edina, Minnesota 55435 • 1-800-800-1312 • fax: 1-952-831-1632